Petal and Poppy and the Spooky Halloween!

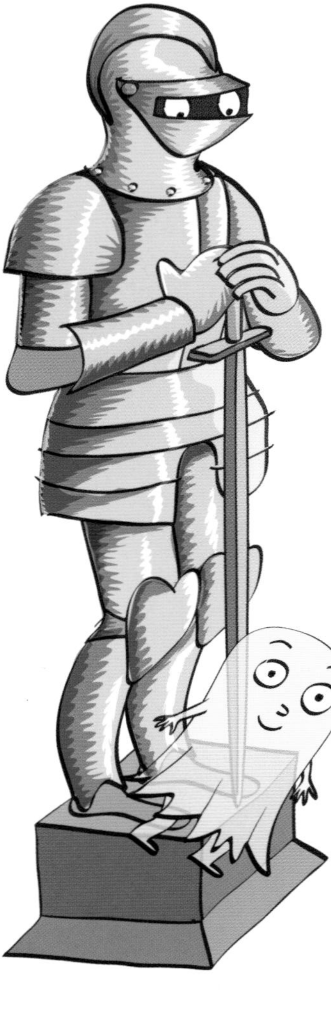

By Lisa Clough
and
Ed Briant

Green Light Readers
Houghton Mifflin Harcourt
Boston New York

www.hmhco.com

The text of this book is set in Cheltenham.
The display type was hand-lettered.
The illustrations were created digitally.

The Library of Congress Cataloging-in-Publication Data is on file.

ISBN: 978-0-544-33603-2 paperback
ISBN: 978-0-544-33602-5 paper over board

Manufactured in China
SCP 10 9 8 7 6 5 4 3 2 1

4500468969

I will spook Petal.

WOOO-HAH-HAH-HAH-HAH-HAH-HAH!

GAAA!

It is me. Poppy!

See?

You are
spooky!

It is only a costume.
GAA!
But it is still me. See?
Where is your party costume?
I do not have one.

Everyone wears a costume.
Not me. I am a scaredy-cat.
You do not have to wear a scary costume.
Can I be a butterfly?

Yes. We can make wings.

Now add glitter.
Lots of glitter!

Ready to go?
Yes!

A perfect night.

All the ghouls are out.
GAAH!

Do not be a scaredy-cat.
They are only costumes.

AHHHHHHHHH!
POP!

GAAAAAA!

Uh-oh!
What will we do!?

Maybe someone in there can help.
In that spooky house?

Do not be such a scaredy-cat.
KNOCK KNOCK!
Hello? Anybody home?
CREAK...
They must not hear us.

We have a flat!
This place is too spooky for me.
CREAK...

Wait here. I will find help.
Hurry back.

I hope there is nothing scary in there!

I hope there is nothing scary out here!

Hello?

GAA!

WHISH, WHISH, WHISH.
Wh . . . wh . . . who is there?

Rattle, rattle, rattle.
CLANK!
GAAA!

Dum-de-dum...

Oooo...ooooo!

I am not a scaredy-cat.

BOO!
It is only a costume.
BEWARE! HAUNTED HOUSE
What are you doing here?
My friend went to get help.
I can help.

Hmmm.

GAAA!
CREEEEEEAK!

GAAAAAAA!
A monster!

GAAA!
CLANGGG!

GAAA!

GAAA!

Petal! This house really is haunted!
BEWARE!

GAAH! A ghost!
BOO!

We fixed the tire.
Great. Time to get out of here!

HOP ON!

Bye-bye.

Are we still going to the party?
I am too scared.

Do not be a scaredy-cat. It is only a costume.

Here.
You do not have to wear a scary costume.
You can be a butterfly . . .
. . . and I will be a monster.

GAA!

It is still me.

HALLOWEEN
PARTY

12

BOO!

They are only costumes!